Carrots Can Dance

Story and illustrations by

Jean Powers

To order additional copies of this book, contact:
Xlibris
1-888-795-4274
www.Xlibris.com
Orders@Xlibris.com

To Reagan, Jordan, Ethan
and Anne, who inspired this book

2

Hi Grandma!

4

We are here today

with you in the garden

to dig

and play.

Last night it rained

(Did you hear it?)

and look what's left,

drops of dew

for me to check.

Remember...

we planted seeds

in the Spring?

Now, see the food

we can bring

in the house

to cook and eat

a dinner together.

That's a treat!

Time to look at

your garden now.

What do we pick?

What do we dig?

Grandma, show us how.

Here's a pea pod

that is fat and green.

Maybe ...

it's the biggest I've seen.

13

"Time to pick the peas,"
you say.

Should I pinch off the top
this way?

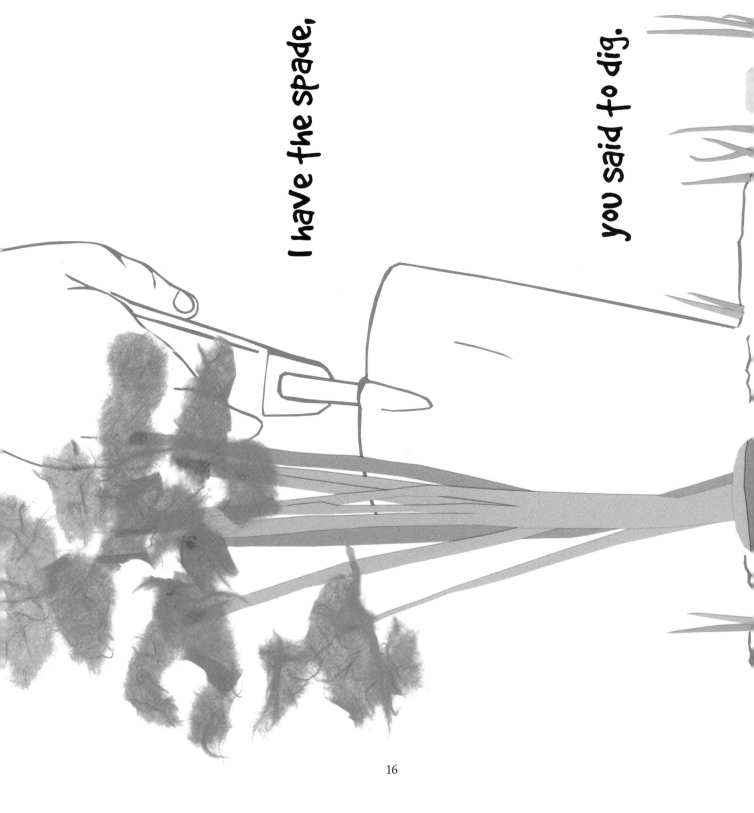

I have the spade,

you said to dig.

Down,

Down,

Down...

wow, this one is big!

Carrots are ready to dig.

Let's go.

I touch the fluffy tops

just so.

I can make them dance!

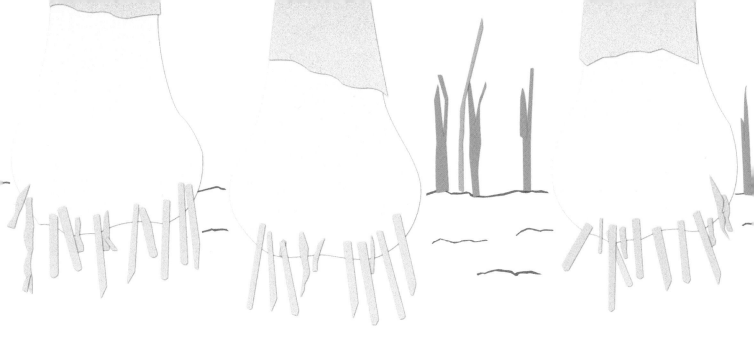

onions are close,

just underground.

Their stalks are

tall,

thin

and round.

Next, there's broccoli on a stalk,

over here – not far to walk.

You know how to cut

this just right,

so we can eat it up tonight.

Grandma, see...it looks like a TREE!

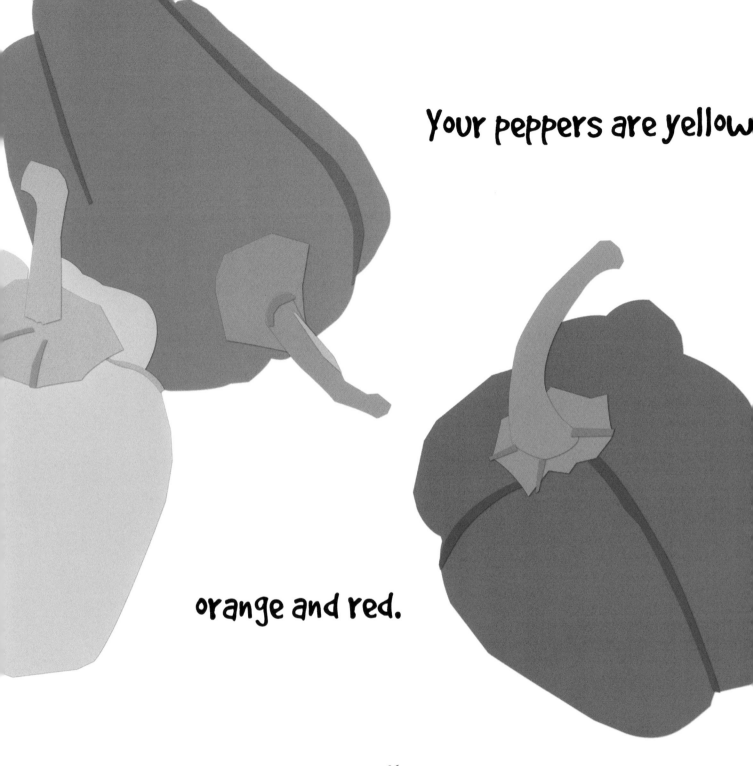

Your peppers are yellow,

orange and red.

"These are the ones to pick,"

you said.

Beans,

tomatoes

and squash,

we get them;

one by one,

gardening with Grandma,

our day is almost done.

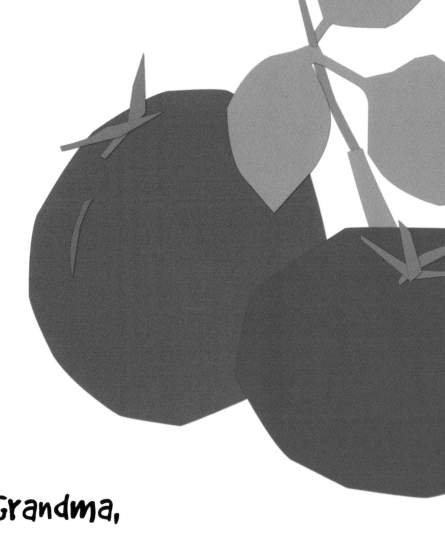

Now we have yummy

food to bring home.

And tomorrow

even more will have grown.

Before we eat

one more place to go

over here,

Look! OH!

29

flowers, flowers,
their colors are bright

et's pick these for the table tonight.

Some are short,

some are tall.

Some smell sweet or

not at all.

Pink, yellow, purple, blue...

I like them ALL and so do you.

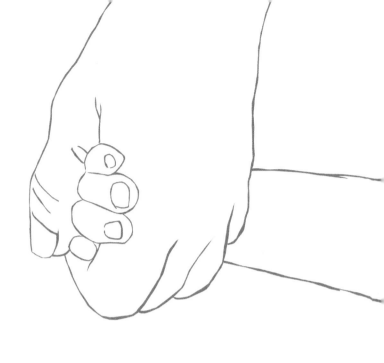
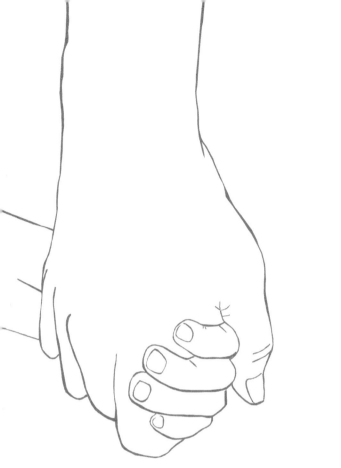

Thank you, Grandma,

for helping us today,

play and discover

in the garden this way.

Race you

to the house!

CPSIA information can be obtained at www.ICGtesting.com
Printed in the USA
LVIW01n2130260616
494212LV00006B/10

* 9 7 8 1 5 1 4 4 8 9 2 7 7 *